HEARSAY

PERFORMANCE POEMS PLUS

Compiled by
Paul Beasley

A Red Fox Book

Published by Random House Children's Books
20 Vauxhall Bridge Road, London SW1V 2SA

A division of Random House UK Ltd
London Melbourne Sydney Auckland
Johannesburg and agencies throughout the world

1 3 5 7 9 10 8 6 4 2

First published by The Bodley Head Children's Books 1994

Red Fox edition 1995

Printed and bound in Great Britain by
The Guernsey Press Co. Ltd, Vale, Guernsey, C.I.

RANDOM HOUSE UK Limited Reg. No 954009

ISBN 0 09 930362 0

◈ CONTENTS ◈

◈ INTRODUCTION ◈

For a good while now I've been involved in organizing shows for poets, or rather for people to come and hear poets present their work. It's been exciting listening not only to what the poets have to say but *how* they say it — with many of them working in ways which move between the poem on the page and its performance, so putting a fresh emphasis on the spoken word.

This book is inspired by this popular movement in poetry, often coming under the banner of 'performance poetry', and so the title — *Hearsay* — and an anthology which asks to be read aloud. Of course these poems can be read silently to yourself, but they also invite you to try them on your tongue — for size and shape, for texture and taste! They can be heard, not only with your mind's ear but with your real physical head-gear, and so shared with others in all kinds of ways and settings.

There are a lot of poems here that revel in sound-play and patterning, upfront in their use of rhythm, rhyme and other special sonic effects. Some are altogether musically inspired, riding on rap, reggae and jazzy rhythms, rock and bhangra beats, just as others feel out their own unique lyrical forms.

You'll hear a lot of different voices, all with their own manners, moods and attitudes. Some wildly funny, some deadly serious, some ironic. And you'll pick up on a range of dialects — from broad Yorks to Scots and Irish brogue, from Jamaican patois to standard and American English — all of them in some sense with an accent, local and vocal.

Irresistibly, many themes surface through and alongside the subject of language, perhaps especially questions of identity, like what makes us different and what we have in common; also relationships — between the sexes, across cultures and generations. The encounter of these borders and passages, and their crossing, echoes throughout the book.

You might say this book would be better off being a cassette, a video or even a night out at a show, and you'd be right — I'd only add that it is! A lot of these poets are now making recordings of all sorts, and perhaps more importantly, performing their work in venues such as music and theatre spaces, youth clubs and schools. Some are probably coming live to a venue near you soon and if not, you can always invite them.

Paul Beasley

ACKNOWLEDGEMENTS

The compiler and publishers would like to thank the following people for giving permission to include in this anthology material which is their copyright. The publishers have made every effort to trace copyright holders. If we have inadvertently omitted to acknowledge anyone we should be most grateful if this could be brought to our attention for correction at the first opportunity.

Bloodaxe for 'Overstanding' by Benjamin Zephaniah (*City Psalms* 1992); Mandarin for 'Poetry', and Andre Deutsch for 'Untitled' by John Hegley (*Can I Come Down Now Dad?* 1992. *Glad to wear Glasses* 1990 resp.); Bogle L'Ouverture for 'Everything Is Rhythmical' by Lemn Sissay (*Tender Fingers In A Clenched Fist* 1988); Outposts Poetry Quarterley for 'From Silence' by Debjani Chatterjee; Virago Press for 'A Song To Heal', and Race Today Publications. 'For soun de abeng fi nanny' and 'dreamer' by Jean 'Binta' Breeze (*Spring Cleaning* 1992, *Riddym Ravings* 1988 resp.); Anvil Press for 'Away and See' and 'River' by Carol Ann Duffy (*Mean Time* 1993, *The Other Country* 1990 resp.); New Beacon Books for 'Some Of My Worst Wounds' and 'Blue Peace Incantation' by Lorna Goodison (*Heartease* 1988); The Wide Skirt Press for 'Proving Weak And True' by Martin Stannard (*Denying England* 1989); Sun Tavern Fields for 'You Make Me So Nervous' by Fran Landesman (*The Thorny Side of Love* 1992); Peters, Fraser & Dunlop and Viking Press for 'Planet Babel' by Roger McGough (*Defying Gravity* 1992); Eatlatinandie Books for 'Tennis' by Emile Sercombe (*Forty Best Performance Poems* 1984); Label Magazine and Twist In The Tail for 'Mime Doesn't Pay' and 'The Poem Within You' by Henry Normal (*Issue 8* 1988 and *The Third Person* 1993 resp.); Centreprise for 'If You Think' by Lotte Moos (*Time to be Bold* 1981); Scholastic Children's Books for 'How Many' and 'Grammar' by Mike Rosen (*Mind The Gap* 1992); Cambridge Press and Bogle L'Ouverture for 'Tables' and 'Language Barrier' by Val Bloom (*Duppy Jamboree* 1992, and *Touch mi, tell mi!* 1993 resp.); Virago Press for 'Wha Me Mudder Do' and 'We New World Blacks' by Grace Nichols (*Lazy Thoughts Of A Lazy Woman* 1989, *The Fat Black Woman's Poems* 1984); Rogers, Coleridge & White and Paladin for 'The Mule's Favourite Dream' by Brian Patten (*Grinning Jack* 1992); Blackie Books for 'A Change of Scene' by John Mole (*The Conjuror's Rabbit* 1992); Jonathan Cape for 'An African Elegy' by Ben Okri (*An*

African Elegy 1992); Bogle L'Ouverture for 'Pounding Rice' and 'A "Coloured" Girl, I Sleep With Rainbows' by Lucinda Roy (*Wailing the Dead to Sleep* 1988); Crocus Books for 'Talking To My Father' by Pat Amick (*She Says* 1988); Virago Press, The Women's Press and Karia Press for 'Some Days, Mother', 'You Carry My Life' and 'Behind Shutters' by Merle Collins (*Rotten Pomerack* 1992, *Rain Darling* 1991, *Because The Dawn Breaks* 1985 resp.); Basement Writers Publishing for 'Strong As A Lion' and 'When Your Voice Breaks' by Sean Taylor (*Take It From Me* 1992); Blackie Books for 'Brendon Gallacher' by Jackie Kay (*Two's Company* 1992); Polygon Press for 'The Message', 'The Visitors' and 'The Warning' by Brian McCabe (*One Atom to Another* 1987); Arena Books for 'for, i wanna be yours' and 'i don't wanna be nice' by John Cooper Clarke (*ten years in an open necked shirt* 1983); Windows Merseyside Poetry for 'Law Of Opposites' by Levi Tarafi (*Duboetry* 1988); Bloodaxe/LKJ for 'Sense Outta Nansense' by Linton Kwesi Johnson (*Tings an Times* 1991); the Blackstaff Press for 'Nothing for Girls' by Maighread Medbh (*The Making of a Pagan* 1990); Salmon Publishing for 'End of a Free Ride' and 'Be Someone' by Rita Ann Higgins (*Witch in the Bushes* 1988); The Poetry Review 1993 for 'Yes' by Adrian Mitchell; Puffin Books and Pluto Press for 'How Laughter Helped Stop The Argument' and 'Cowtalk' by John Agard (*Laughter is an Egg* 1991, *Mangoes & Bullets* 1985 resp.); Laura Cecil and Faber & Faber for 'This Poem' by Norman Silver (*The Comic Shop* 1993).

The following poems are being published for the first time in this anthology and appear by permission of their authors unless otherwise stated. All these poems are copyright © 1994 by the authors:

'Dance' by Jean Buffong; 'Hungry Ghost' by Debjani Chatterjee; 'Yorkshire Language Day' by Ian McMillan & Martyn Wiley; 'Names' and 'Attention Seeking' by Jackie Kay; 'Nice Man' and 'When You're Old' by Nick Toczek; 'Fourth Generation' by Maya Chowdhry; and 'Blue Coffee' and 'A Flying Song' by Adrian Mitchell.

OVERSTANDING

Open up yu mind mek some riddim cum in
Open up yu brain do some reasoning
Open up yu thoughts so we can connect
Open up fe knowledge an intellect.
Open up de speaker mek we blast de sound
Open up de sky mek de Bass cum down
Open up yu eyes mek we look inside
If yu need fe overstand dis open wide.

Open up yu house mek de Refugee cum in
Yu may overstand an start helping
Open yu imagination, gu fe a ride
If yu want fe overstand dis open wide

Open up yu fiss an welcum a kiss
Getta loada dis open up business
Open up yu Bank Account an spend
Open up yu wallet an check a fren.
Open up de dance floor mek I dance
Open up yu body an luv romance
If yu have not opened up, yu hav not tried
See de other side an open wide

Open up de border free up de land
Open up de books in de Vatican
Open up yu self to any possibility
Open up yu heart an yu mentality.
Open any door dat yu confront
Let me put it straight, sincere and blunt
Narrow mindedness mus run an hide
Fe a shot of overstanding
Open Wide.

Benjamin Zephaniah

Poetry

poetry don't have to be
living in a library
there's poetry that you can see
in the life of everybody,
a lick of paint's the kind of thing I mean
a lick of paint's a lovely piece of writing
the tongue of the paintbrush
giving something drab
a dab new sheen
a lick of paint's exciting.

there are folk who like to see
Latin in their poetry
and plenty of obscurity
me for instance
(only joking)
how I like to listen to the lingo
in bingo
legs eleven
clickety-click
a lick of paint
no — sorry that ain't one

poetry — language on a spree
I want to be
a leaf on the poetree
poetry is good for me
I think I'll have some for my tea

John Hegley

◇ ◇ untitled

it's hard to make a conscience out of custard
it's hard to hear things when they're very faint
things look cleaner when they've just been dusted
unless it's done with absolute restraint
a missing person's rarely called Xavier
public houses have no patron saint
you'd think they would have canonised the saviour
he'll be coming back and lodging a complaint
if you're somebody who tends to go and burgle
middle class you generally ain't
it's hard to keep your gob shut when you gurgle
especially when you're gurgling with paint
the best words don't sound much with bad diction
the pave meant very little to the kerb
a phone bill without figures is a fiction
a gerbil without illness is a gerb

John Hegley

The Imagination

the only nation worth defending
a nation without alienation
a nation whose flag is invisible
and whose borders are forever beyond the horizon
a nation whose currency is the idea
whose sole weapon is the idea
and whose badge is a chrysanthemum of sweet wrappings
maybe
a nation whose motto is why have one or the other
when you can have one the other and both
a nation whose customs are not barriers
whose uniform is multiform
whose anthem is improvised
whose enemies are losing
whose export is truth
and whose poetry does not have many laughs

John Hegley

PINK
POEM

pink is the colour
of shrimps and prawn cocktails
and bridesmaids
and milkshakes
and lip gloss
and bedrooms
and candy floss
and curtains
and sponge bags
and ribbons
and roses
and carpets
carnations
and love letters
botties
and brassières
and bog rolls
and babies
blancmanges
and sugar mice
and icing
and lampshades
and pink is, apparently, for women.

pink is the colour
of sweeties and cakies
and duvets

and bed sheets
and knickers
and nighties
and slippers
and pillows
of sweetness
and lightness
and neatness
and niceness
of smiling and smiling
and waiting and waiting
of angora jumpers
and unhappy poodles
and bonnets
and sashes
and rashes
and pearls
pink is the colour
of puddingy softness
and pink is, apparently, for girls.

pink is the colour
of nothing and no one
anaemic and wasted
synthetic and cheap
of bland invitations
to tupperware parties
of tutus and bootees
and velvet settees

it's wishy and washy
and squishy and squashy
a pulsating puddle
of Angel Delight
a coagulation
of strawberry sundaes —
the colour she wears
on a Saturday night
a watery sunset
a bilious twinset
a hideous mixture
of blood-red and white

pink is the colour
of things that don't matter
of things that don't move
and that don't make a noise
it's the colour for grannies
and cute little girlies
but never, no never, for boys.

it's the colour of twaddle
the colour of pap
the colour of sweet valentines
full of soft little bunnies
and romantic crap
and poems with terrible rhymes

 it's a mixture of giblets
and seething whale blubber
as worn by the Royals
and Prime Ministers' wives
and Women's Guild members
and miserable aunties
and people with monotone lives
who like to sniff Omo
and snort Evostick
and get a real kick out of Shake 'N' Vac
and say
'Pink is the colour for women, my dear.'

No wonder I like to wear black.

Ann Ziety

Scrunge Shrimpkin
at the bottom of the ooze
lived on globularis
swollen with mud
pumped up with sloop
and sloppy despicables
    but I loved him

Scrunge Shrimpkin
pottled around on the river's slimy mattress
wallowed in ancient nasties
gorged his shovel-mouth with shrivelled death
and snored
like a motorbike throbbing over a cattle-grid

    but I loved him nonetheless

he lummered over the encrusted scum
like a scaley sea-adder, frothy-mouthed
full of gastric fumes and fish oil
fashioned in filth
sieving seaweed seed pods through his gut
knitting grey humus out of algae-smothered crisp packets
wrinkled in the sog
Scrunge Shrimpkin pissed on his own foot
    but I loved him

    and it wasn't easy

'Hey Scrunge!' the kids used to shout
'He's got odd socks on!'
and Scrunge would slither back
in deep
down
faster than falling
and fasten his bulk onto the very bottom bog
cover his ugly ears with sog-clods
fiddle with his tubes
blow out little spores of sadness
and bellow into the black

at the bottom

vagabond abalones nibbled at his slack skin
the colour of lard
and demon dribblers raked his back
cooked in the bubbling squishy
Scrunge Shrimpkin
was *al dente*
but in the middle of a heave
he blew great gobbets of poison
at the skinny pilchards
and squirmed into the slush
safe
and sound

Scrunge Shrimpkin
made a hole
in the glaucous, soft hills
combed his tendrils tickled with daphnia
snored
like a manatee with adenoids
and was buried at the bottom of the world

    but I loved him

Ann Ziety

everything is
rhythmical

Rhythm Rhythm
Can you
Hear the
Rhythms

Quick rhythm
Slow rhythm
God given
Life giving

Rhythm rhythm
Can you
Hear the
Rhythms rhythms

If you listen close
Ears to the ground
The basis of noise
Is rhythm sound
From spoken words to ways of walk
From rappin' to reggae and funk we talk in

Rhythm rhythm
Can you
Hear the
Rhythms

Way back in the heart of Africa
They took our drums away
But rhythm proved its own power
By being here today

All four corners these sweet-sounding rhythms
reach
With treble in the speaker even bass in the speech
To the freezing cold and heat in heights
Muhammad Ali did do it in his fights
With

Rhythm rhythm
Can you
Hear the
Rhythms

Quick rhythms
Slick rhythms
Bold rhythms
Gold rhythms

God giving
Life giving
Rhythms

Rhythms

Can you
Hear the

Lemn Sissay

dance

Thud thud thump
       they bash their drums
Voices shriek out mumbled words
Faces as hard
       eyes as cold as a winter's night
Wooden bodies shift about like robots.

Don't you dance? they ask

Of course we dance
We dance to the music
We dance to the rhythm
Music that touches the soul
Music that stirs the heart
Music that vibrates across the mountain tops.

Boom a boom a boompity boom
       the drums shout out
Ping zing ping a ling ting
       the steel pan and guitar echoes
Phew pheewp pheew pheewp the flute joins in

A boom a boom a ping zing a ling pheewp
       a boompity boom,
They mingle
       they tingle
               they tangle,

Then the eyes laugh
       the face beams
The feet tap a rap a tap
       they tease the body
Together they dance and they dance,

Yes we do know how to dance
Do YOU?

Jean Buffong

FROM SILENCE

'Speech is . . . but silence is golden.'
'Little girls should be seen, not heard.'
What bully shut our silver mouths?
('In the beginning was the Word.')

Silence is ripening, yearning,
listening. Let my silence grow —
silence to nurture thoughtful speech.
From silence may my language flow.

Debjani Chatterjee

Hungry Ghost

Today I went shopping with my father
after many years. I felt I was back
in time to when I'd follow grandfather
to the market, smelling the spicy scents,
drinking the sights and mingling with the shouts.
Neither buyer nor seller, I would float
like a restless spirit, hungry for life.

The market is bigger. I have grown too.
There are more goods as distances have shrunk.
The prices are higher. I understand
about money and, alas, its bondage
of buyers and sellers. Almost I wish
I was again that hungry ghost, watchful
and floating through the world's noisy bazaar.

Debjani Chatterjee

a song to heal

she walk
to de riddym
a de heartbeat
talk
like a rustling wind
touch
like cool spring water
distant
as de land of dreams

      an no one knows

how she does
    as she waits
an waits
    as she does

watching de sky
for rain
heart strung
like a quiet scream

      an no one knows

how night
grow into morning
out of a creeping dusk
an wake yuh
in a cruel moment
too naked
for an eye to throw a blind
on pain
for calm
in de centre
a de hurricane
    no one knows

an she prays
    as she writes

an writes
    as she prays
for de calm
    of de touch of understanding
for a word for de eagle
    an de dove

for a song so real
a song to heal
        no one knows

how she waits
    as she does
an does
    as she waits
waits as she prays
    an prays
as she writes
        den she rise
        an she sing
        an sing
        as she rise

chanting to de riddym a de heartbeat
talking like a rustling wind
touching like cool spring water
distant as de land of dreams
distant
as de land of dreams

Jean 'Binta' Breeze

soun de abeng fi nanny

Nanny siddung pon a rack
a plan a new attack
puffin pon a red clay pipe

an de campfire
staat to sing

wile hog a spit grease
pon machete crease
sharp as fire release
an er yeye roam crass
ebery mountain pass
an er yeas well tune to de win'

an de cricket an de treefrog
crackle telegram
an she wet er battam lip fi decode

an de people gadda roun
tune een to er soun
wid a richness dat aboun
she wear dem crown
pon er natty platty atless head

an ebery smoke fram er pipe
is a signal fi de fight
an de people dem a sing
mek de cockpit ring
an de chant jus a rise, jus a rise
to de skies

wid de fervour of freedom
dat bus up chain
dat stap de ceaseless itching
of de sugar cane

We sey wi nah tun back
we a bus a new track
dutty tuff
but is enuff
fi a bite
fi wi fight

an ebery shake of a leaf
mek dem quiver
mek dem shiver
fa dem lose dem night sight
an de daylight too bright
an we movin like de creatures of de wile
we movin in a single file
fa dis a fi we fightin style

an de message reach crass
ebery mountain pass

we sey wi nah tun back
we a bus a new track
dutty tuff
but is enuff
fi a bite
fi wi fight

life well haad
mongs de wattle an de daub
eben de dankey
a hiccup
in im stirrup
for de carrot laas it class
so nuh mek no one come faas
eena wi business

dis a fi we lan
a yah we mek wi stan

mongs de tuff dutty gritty
dis yah eart nah show no pity
less yuh
falla fashion
home een like pigeon
an wear dem number like de beas
but wen yuh see er savage pride
yuh haffi realise
dat

wi nah tun back
wi a bus a new track
dutty tuff
but is enuff
fi a bite
fi we fight
dutty tuff
but is enuff
is enuff

so mek wi soun de abeng
fi Nanny

Jean 'Binta' Breeze

dreamer

  roun a rocky corner
by de sea
seat up
  pon a drif wood
yuh can fine she
gazin cross de water
a stick
  eena her han
trying to trace
    a future
  in de san

Jean 'Binta' Breeze

river

At the turn of the river the language changes,
a different babble, even a different name
for the same river. Water crosses the border,
translates itself, but words stumble, fall back,
and there, nailed to a tree, is proof. A sign

in new language brash on a tree. A bird,
not seen before, singing on a branch. A woman
on the path by the river, repeating a strange sound
to clue the bird's song and ask for its name, after.
She kneels for a red flower, picks it, later
will press it carefully between the pages of a book.

What would it mean to you if you could be
with her there, dangling your own hands in the water
where blue and silver fish dart away over stone,
stoon, stein, like the meanings of things, vanish?
She feels she is somewhere else, intensely, simply
    because
of words; sings loudly in nonsense, smiling, smiling.

If you were really there what would you write on a
    postcard,
or on the sand, near where the river runs into the sea?

Carol Ann Duffy

AWAY AND SEE

Away and see an ocean suck at a boiled sun
and say to someone things I'd blush even to dream.
Slip off your dress in a high room over the harbour.
Write to me soon.

New fruits sing on the flipside of night in a market
of language, light, a tune from the chapel nearby
stopping you dead, the peach in your palm respiring.
Taste it for me.

Away and see the things that words give a name to, the
    flight
of syllables, wingspan stretching a noun. Test words
wherever they live; listen and touch, smell, believe.
Spell them with love.

Skedaddle. Somebody chaps at the door at a year's end,
    hopeful.
Away and see who it is. Let in the new, the vivid,
horror and pity, passion, the stranger holding the future.
Ask him his name.

Nothing's the same as anything else. Away and see
for yourself. Walk. Fly. Take a boat till land reappears,
altered forever, ringing its bells, alive. Go on. G'on. Gon.
Away and see.

Carol Ann Duffy

some of my worst wounds

Some of my worst wounds
have healed into poems.
A few well placed
stabs in the back
have released a singing
trapped between my shoulders.
A carrydown
has lent leverage
to the tongue's rise
and betrayals sent words
hurrying home
to toe the line again.

Lorna Goodison

blue peace
incantation

Within blue of peace,
the azure of calm,
beat soft now bright heart,
beat soft, sound calm.
By cobalt of love deep
indigo of perception
by waters of sky blue
by need's incantation
be measured
blue measured
in verdant balance
of green
heart be rocked calm now
light we have seen.
By meditations of
clear waters,
all strivings cease,
within all,
illumination,
forever, lasting blue peace.

Lorna Goodison

Proving Weak and True

Music from a distance can be beautiful,
as can sunsets by the sea and
cottages nestled among green valleys.
Laughter from a playground is pretty nice,
and the happy yapping of dogs.
Reaching the brow of a hill is good,
looking down and tracing the line of a road
as it meanders off into the distance,
and a cool refreshing tumbler of water
can scarcely be bettered.
Bonfire smoke on an early autumn evening
is redolent of nature's robustness,
and a woman wheeling her new baby
along the street is inspiring.
Furry animals are pleasing to children,
and bathtime is especially good
for an archaeologist friend of mine.
Newly-baked bread is a delight, and
even its smell sets the taste buds alight;
bacon has the same effect, and is
probably holy in certain households.
Tears well up in the eyes at the sight
of well-deserved success, and the family
gathered together for a special occasion
should be savoured for what it is.
The scent of flowers filling a room
makes the day, as does a letter
from someone you thought you had lost.
Brilliant colours in dreams are a sign
of affirmation, and a kiss on the cheek
says more than a thousand words.

Martin Stannard

you make me
so nervous

You make me so nervous
You make me so tense
I snap and I stammer
It doesn't make sense

You make me so nervous
I talk much too fast
And when we're both happy
I'm scared it won't last

The pleasure you give me at moments
Is more than my pen can express
But why do you give me the feeling
That I'm such a terrible mess

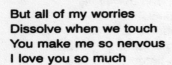

When you're in a bad mood
You make me so sad
I simply can't bear it
You're driving me mad

But all of my worries
Dissolve when we touch
You make me so nervous
I love you so much

Fran Landesman

Planet Babel

'I found I could not use the long line because of my nervous nature.'

William Carlos Williams

As soon as my voice is heard above the babble
Which ceases as people turn
I want to disappear. Hide under the table.

My pulse races and I consequently gabble.
Puzzled faces make mine burn
And make it crystal clear – I'm from Planet Babel.

Roger McGough

● Tennis

An action poem for one, two or more players. The server plays from the left, the receiver from the right of the margin. The shots are in *italics*. The umpire rules in UPPER CASE; the crowd chants in (brackets); the commentator is **bold** when the rain falls.

Patter swinger *pop*, zooch torpedo fires is good
    skid *bong*, marge scrape blossom swish spread
smack, steel cross-cut teethstips
    stretchout *pang*, scarce scramble eggover
quick *slash*, crafty widdle trick
    skip *stun*, word weight
bonk-eh, elbow hefty
    ponk, poo
plop, moon pale ghost ball
    rocket, head height hurl
hits, off wood jinx bits sidespun
    oh, sliced soft
sop, comes wings lightning and
    soft *sop*, and
sop, back and
    pat-back
pat-again
    whack-back
smack
    smash
flummoxed
    standstill
frowns
    smiles
            LOVE IS STEAM
Prom pom diddle, arcs up teeters, *poing*, dresden delft deft
    crash, pieces best teaset snap, goes away
            LOVE IS MURKY

eh was non allowed in unleaven ball, flubbed oud
                    GOOZGOG
dead
                    PLAY
no sod it stupid soggy lump, he hit it out
        SOUND AS GOOZGOG, PLAY ON
Noselunk salunk awk sulk, whinnie referee, whinnie see
my mum
            THIS IS A SNUBLICK WARBLING
        (bray all, all bray, bray bray, bray bray bray
            haw haw haw hoof stomp
            bray haw bray haw bray haw
                clomp clomp clomp)
it, stompond ground stand, inner pound
sterling right self, deaf fie ain't
                    PLAYON
it

                    PLAAAYYON
nope
LAZER TIGHT HIGH NOTE, SPITSHARP DIAMOND
                CLEARPITCH
FAST AS A BLUEBOLT, WAVE SPLITTING
            KINGFISHER SHEARING
            PSSSSSSSSHUNK
psshally wunk old blueblack bottle
bombing big bellied flop in the kid's end
fester gemthing and rustic asspot
            ONE POINT AGAINST YOU
            LOVE IS NAUGHTY
        lissen, keep your trap shut out there
shovvel monkey mug, squeeze up like rotten orange it!
cool lid, pour oil, slow slide bike ride backwards
well ok, ok . . .
 promp a tomp a tomp, sssssssss ssslash sssslash
slash smash slash smash slash smash slash smash
    million cold aces piss straight down, unzip air
        watchers clustering flying falling
        helpless struck and slaughtered
as stains spread across seats and water crowns
                    dance
jets smash flesh wood concrete glass grass gingham

**into darkness, strike cartons to sog
liquidize bread and cheese to pigeon shit
drown a low level dog
after six hours, leaves off
rainbow, sunnout, steams**
                    PLAY
pace up pat up, unwinds, *fut*, fissile missle
    bop, and stumble stop shot, cough drop
bang waggon, sax break, earwincer
    pounder streaky greenback, family pack
splashout, butt and froth, spill flood
    dam, long boulder bouncer founder
bonk, low slung blow shin shatterer
    slice, early curly vasive, wrist swing splitter
gawp, gasp angled banner fangled
    ssing, birds on lark song
flashacross, hack elastic whirlmagic
    swang, two hands, skid scollop sky dollop
prang, granite, zonk, zonk, zonk
                    OUT

    hooray!
            IT'S GRIM SAT IN A MARSH
grannys crumble, burnt, bitter, rejected
full of venge

Emile Sercombe

MIME DOESN'T PAY

Last night I was burgled by a mime artist. He never made a sound. He could have got away with it, but then he tried to steal a piano I haven't got. He pushed and pulled, strained and heaved, but it wouldn't budge. Maybe he thought there was something valuable behind it. There wasn't. He tried to float the piano. He blew up a balloon, tied it to the piano, then couldn't lift the balloon. I found him in the morning trapped inside an imaginary box. I called the police. He started to panic. He tried climbing up a fictitious ladder. When the police arrived they let him out. He made a dash for it. Tried running away on the spot. It took the police two hours to get him into the car; he kept getting pulled back by an invisible rope. I decided not to press charges. This afternoon I put in an insurance claim for the piano.

Henry Normal

The Poem Within You

Opened to the coldness of the room
Is the poem deep inside you
You shrug and faint dismissal
But it is as you'd hoped
It is your poem
Private and sacred
It belongs to you alone
Guarded and enshrined
It is the very heart of you
You are concerned for its progress
You are both embarrassed and proud
And in an act of defiance
In an act of pure humanity
You hold out your poem
Sure that it has its place
Opened to the coldness of the room
Is the poem deep inside you
And for a moment the room is warmed
And in that moment you are content
And in a world of such poems
How can anyone die lonely and cold?

Henry Normal

IF YOU THINK

If you think
Blows
Struck in Ireland
Won't hurt you
Think again
They will hurt you
If you think
The knife
Slid between the ribs of a Pakistani
Will glance off your lighter skin
Think again

If you think
Bullets hissing towards beating hearts
In some country we know nothing about
Will miss you
Think again
They will not miss your beating heart

If you think
Needles
Jabbed into veins
To make the blood run docile
Won't prick you
Think again

They will hurt you, hit you, prick you
And they will not miss you
We are all one
One trembling human flesh

Lotte Moos

how
many

(for Mordecai Vanunu)

how many people
who know
don't say?

How many people
who say,
don't say it all?

how many people
who say it all,
don't get heard?

how many people
who get heard
get rubbed out?

how many people
who get rubbed out,
get forgotten?

how many people
remember the ones
they want us to forget?

Mike Rosen

grammar

The teacher said:
A noun is a naming word.
What is the naming word in the sentence:
'He named the ship *Lusitania*?
'Named', said George.
Wrong, it's 'ship'.
Oh, said George.

The teacher said:
A verb is a doing word.
What is the doing word in the sentence:
'I like doing homework'?
'Doing', said George.
Wrong, it's 'like'.
Oh, said George.

The teacher said:
An adjective is a describing word.
What is the describing word in the sentence:
'Describing sunsets is boring'?
'Describing', said George.
Wrong, it's 'boring'.
I know it is, said George.

Mike Rosen

tables

Headmaster a come, Mek has'e! Sit down
— Amy! Min' yuh bruck Jane collar-bone,
Tom! Tek yuh foot off o' de desk,
Sandra Wallace, mi know yuh vex
But beg yuh get up off o' Joseph head.
Tek de lizard off o' Sue neck, Ted!
Sue, mi dear, don' bawl so loud;
Thomas, yuh can tell mi why yuh put de toad
Eena Elvira sandwich bag?
An Jim, whey yuh a do wid dat bull-frog?
Tek i' off mi table! Yuh mad?
Mi know yuh chair small, May, but it no dat bad
Dat yuh haffe siddung pon de floor!
Jim, don' squeeze de frog unda de door,
Put i' through de window — no, no, Les!
Mi know yuh hungry, but Mary yeas
Won' full yuh up, so spit it out.
Now go wash de blood outa yuh mout'.
Hortense, tek Mary to de nurse.
Nick, tek yuh han out o' Mary purse!
Ah wonda who tell all o' yuh
Sey dat dis class-room is a zoo?
Quick! Headmaster comin' through de door
' — *Two ones are two, two twos are four . . .*'

Valerie Bloom

LANGUAGE
barrier

Jamaica language sweet yuh know bwoy,
An yuh know mi nebba notice i',
Till tarra day one foreign frien'
Come spen some time wid mi.

An den im call mi attention to
Some tings im sey soun' queer,
Like de way wi always sey 'koo yah'
When we really mean 'look here'.

Den annodda ting whey puzzle im,
Is how wi lub 'repeat' wise'f
For de ongle time im repeat a wud
Is when smaddy half deaf.

Todda day im a walk outa road
An when im a pass one gate,
Im see one bwoy a one winda,
An one nodda one outside a wait.

Im sey dem did look kine o' nice
Soh im ben a go sey howdy,
But im tap shart when de fus' bwoy sey
'A ready yuh ready aready?'

Den like sey dat ney quite enuff,
Fe po' likkle foreign Hugh,
Him hear de nedda bwoy halla out,
'A come mi come fe come wait fe yuh.'

An dat is nat all dat puzzle him,
Why wi run wi words togedda?
For when im expec' fe hear 'the other',
Him hear dis one word, 'todda'.

Instead o' wi sey 'all of you'
Wi ongle sey unoo,
Him can dis remember sey
De wud fe 'screech owl' is 'patoo'.

As fe some expression him hear,
Im wouldn badda try meck dem out,
Like 'boonoonoonos, chamba-chamba',
An 'kibba up yuh mout'.

Him can hardly see de connection,
Between 'only' an 'dengey',
An im woulda like fe meet de smaddy
Who invent de wud 'preckey'.

Mi advise im no fe fret imself,
For de Spaniards do it to,
For when dem mean fe sey 'jackass',
Dem always sey 'burro'.

De French, Italian, Greek an Dutch,
Dem all guilty o' de crime
None a dem no chat im language,
Soh Hugh betta larn fe mime.

But sayin' dis an dat yuh know,
Some o' wi cyan eben undastan one anodda,
Eben doah wi all lib yah
An chat de same patois.

For from las' week mi a puzzle out,
Whey Joey coulda mean,
When im teck im facey self soh ax
Ef any o' im undapants clean.

Valerie Bloom

Wha Me Mudder Do

Mek me tell you wha me Mudder do
wha me mudder do
wha me mudder do

Me mudder pound plantain mek fufu
Me mudder catch crab mek calaloo stew

Mek me tell you wha me mudder do
wha me mudder do
wha me mudder do

Me mudder beat hammer
Me mudder turn screw
she paint chair red
then she paint it blue

Mek me tell you wha me mudder do
wha me mudder do
wha me mudder do

Me mudder chase bad-cow
with one 'Shoo'
she paddle down river
in she own canoe
Ain't have nothing
dat me mudder can't do
Ain't have nothing
dat me mudder can't do

Mek me tell you

Grace Nichols

WE NEW WORLD BLACKS

The timbre
in our voice
betrays us
however far
we've been

whatever tongue
we speak
the old ghost
asserts itself
in dusky echoes

like driftwood
traces

and in spite of
ourselves
we know the way
back to

the river stone

the little decayed
spirit
of the navel string
hiding in our back garden

Grace Nichols

YORKSHIRE
LANGUAGE day

It's Yorkshire Language Day
yes Yorkshire Language Day
oh the 28th February every year
is Yorkshire Language Day

Well I say to you
and you say to me
talk reyt
talk proper
talk tha
talk thee
standing at the bus stop
sitting in the club
walking down the high street
drinking in the pub
talk Yorkshire language
old and good
and semmas, tha knows
misunderstood

It's Yorkshire Language Day
yes Yorkshire Language Day
oh the 28th February every year
is Yorkshire Language Day

Call it accent
call it dialect
call it sloppy speech
call it Yorkshire language
Cos tha knows
it's better than a southerner's grating speech

Say bath not barth
say grass not grarse
talking like a Londoner's
a pointless farce

Tha wain't feel leet
that wain't sound low
if tha wobbles thi gob
and let's thi Yorkshire show

Put coil in't coil oil
chuck out sleck
dun't talk like thi clack's
at back o' thi neck

It's Yorkshire Language Day
yes Yorkshire Language Day
oh the 28th February every year
is Yorkshire Language Day

So all over't land
from Bath to Ayr
they'll be talking like us
and taking care
to say good neet
and not good night
and giz a leet
not
can you spare a light
when John Major goes to bed
at Number Ten
he'll say has tha turned leet off
no I'll do it myssen

On Yorkshire Language Day
yes Yorkshire Language Day
oh the 28th February every year
is Yorkshire Language Day

Ian McMillan
and Martyn Wiley

the Mule's Favourite Dream

When the mule sings the birds will fall silent.
From among them they will choose a messenger.
It will fly to the court of the Emperor
And bowing with much decorum
Will complain bitterly.

And the Emperor, who had long ago banished all cages,
Who until that moment had been astonished
By the birds' flight and by their singing,
Will throw open the windows and listening
Will detect in the mule's song
Some flaw of which he is particularly fond,

And he will say to the bird, 'O stupid thing!
Let the mule sing,
For there has come about a need of change,
There is a hunger now, a need
For different things.'

This is the mule's favourite dream.
It's his own invention.
Deep in his brain's warren it blossoms.

Brian Patten

A Change of Scene

I couldn't stay, I couldn't go.
What was it there that held me so
Between the darkness and the light?
Two ghosts who would not leave my sight.

They seemed a mother and her child
Picnicking in a golden field
And not a cloud was in the sky
And nobody was asking why.

I couldn't sleep, I couldn't wake.
It felt as if a storm might break
But not on them, not there, oh no
Not on that scene which held me so

Until it changed, when suddenly
Those ghosts took one last look at me,
The field grew dark, the golden land
Was nothing but a waste of sand.

Nothing but dust stretched on and on,
The mother and her child had gone
And in their place no picnicking
But hunger vaguely wandering,

Millions of mothers crouching there,
Millions of children eating air.
I couldn't go, I had to stay.
It's only dreams that go away

And this was not a dream, I knew.
The day had come, the night was through
And everyone was asking why,
And so was I. And so was I.

John Mole

an african elegy

We are the miracles that God made
To taste the bitter fruit of Time.
We are precious
And one day our suffering
Will turn into the wonders of the earth.

There are things that burn me now
Which turn golden when I am happy.
Do you see the mystery of our pain?
That we bear poverty
And are able to sing and dream sweet things

And that we never curse the air when it is warm
Or the fruit when it tastes so good
Or the lights that bounce gently on the waters?
We bless things even in our pain.
We bless them in silence.

That is why our music is so sweet.
It makes the air remember.
There are secret miracles at work
That only Time will bring forth.
I too have heard the dead singing.

And they tell me that
This life is good
They tell me to live it gently
With fire, and always with hope.
There is wonder here

And there is surprise
In everything that moves unseen.
The ocean is full of songs.
The sky is not an enemy.
Destiny is our friend.

Ben Okri

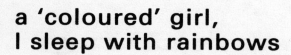

a 'coloured' girl,
I sleep with rainbows

In the belly of the night, when people shed
their skins like snakes and become the cord
that fuses them to fluid dark, I will stand
in prisms of azure and vermilion.
I, a coloured girl with limbs alive with light
will find gold in the cup of my hand
and in the arch of my foot the strength
to bear heaven.

              Nigger is a word of bullet consonants.
In my dreams the word will heal itself —
jagged black letters opening up like children's hands . . .

I am black. I am white.
I am the colour of the sun at noon.
I breathe with the sea.
For coloured girls who sleep with rainbows
there is light in the spittle of strangers.
My father, as black as brown can be;
my mother, as white as the half-moons in his nails.
I am their tangible kiss.

I will see my father
in the painting of my shadow on the earth,
my mother in the light which is the paintbrush.
I will dream again of brilliant distinctions
which span the sky with colour we reach
up and further up to see.

Lucinda Roy

pounding rice

The pole is heavy and she is thirteen
She sees again the comment on her essay, *Excellent*,
And she is suddenly ashamed of her
Filling breasts exposed above the lappa;
She is ashamed of wattle-and-daub huts
Her jigger feet, her pregnancy

Her fingers tighten round the wooden pole;
She pounds the rice in the thick mortar,
Sweats and stabs, looks down past her breasts,
Her rounder belly, and follows the great pole,
Always shattering the delicate grains,
And wishes she had never been to school.

Lucinda Roy

Talking To My Father

I remember the day I turned on you:
'You never showed us love!'

— The only sound was your struggle with
the silicosis, you only seemed to care

about the rhythm of your breathing:
'You never *told* us of your love!'

— 'Towd! Ah wor nivver towd,
burra dint need tellin!'

I pretended not to know
what you were thinking:

— education, the overstimulation of
my brain had made me blind.

Pat Amick

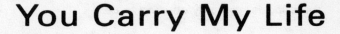

You Carry My Life

you carry my life
in the questions in your eyes
in the silence of your fears
in the anguish of your tears

when you let them stop you walking
my step falters
when you let them stop you talking
my voice becomes weaker
when you let them stop you looking
my eyes grow dimmer
when you let them stop you reasoning
my thoughts become confused
if you think they might stop you
wanting to re-create

look for the rest of us
you carry our lives
in the questions in your eyes
just like we carry yours

Merle Collins

SOME DAYS, MOTHER

Some days, mother
when my thoughts are a tangle I cannot untie
when meanings are lost and I cannot say why
when the day to day drudging is exhausting not fulfilling
when a hollow space inside says I'm existing not living
Those days, mother
when life is a circle that keeps me spinning not moving

Who else in the world could I tell of the pain?
who else in the world could understand the hurt?
Who else in the world would I simply know is sharing?
Who else in the world could so love me in weakness?
Who else, mother? Who else?

Some days, mother
When the coming of morning is an intrusion I fear
When the falling of night fuels thoughts of despair
When prayer for some deeper believing is a passion
I cannot express
When the tolling of time seems so slow and so pointless

Who else in the world could I tell of the hurt?
Who else in the world wouldn't think me insane?
Who else in the world could love me just for
the sake of loving?
Who else, mother, Who else?

Some days, mother
When I can find no meaning even in your existence
When we quarrel and argue and I wish I never knew
    you
When I listen and look and hope I'm not seeing my
    future

When some other searching has fuelled rejection

Who else in the world would love me again without
    question?
Who else holds this feeling that nothing I do can erase?
Who else is simply always there for my story?
Who else, mother? Who else?

Some days, mother,
when I go searching for this kind of loving you're giving
when I go giving this kind of loving you're teaching
It's like trying to hold the rainbow that drinks in the
    river
It's like trying to hug the moonlight that sits on the
doorstep
It's like spinning around in circles and challenging the
    sky
to come falling

So mother, tell me
Who else knows the secret of this deeper loving?
Who else shares the miracle of such tender caring?
Who else is there that knows of this unstinting
    supporting?
Who else, Mother?
Who else?

Merle Collins

BEHIND SHUTTERS

I knew
I had heard it
somewhere before

he said
his father lived
behind shutters
like
'if once
you let yourself care
the crying
might never stop'

and listening
to the printed word
I looked back
over the years
at a face
absorbing the shock
of the idea
of not liking
to be liked

and knew again
the continuing truth
that
whether you admit or not
to caring
once you let yourself
care
for the abstract
or the live

the crying
might never stop

but then again
the joy
might never end

Merle Collins

Strong as a Lion

my Dad's a tree
six foot three
and sometimes
armlocked together
he'd say to me
'I'm as strong as a lion!
How strong am I?'

so I'd reply
'Weak as a FLEA!'

then he'd twist my arm
grinning
and I'd laugh
'Weak as a flea'

and again he'd ask,
eye to eye
'Tell me
how strong am I?'
'Weak as a . . . lion!'
I'd reply

'STRONG as a lion'
he'd insist
giving me
the final twist
and 'Strong as a lion! Yes!'
I'd agree

then a weekend or so ago
as I helped him carry a box
through the snow
he said 'You're strong as a lion'
to me

and he may have said it
because he knows we've changed
or he may have said it
tongue in cheek
or he may have said it
just to make sure
I didn't look him
eye to eye
and ask 'How strong am I?'

Sean Taylor

WHEN YOUR
VOICE BREAKS

they named me
taught me to speak, read and all,
put the words in my mouth for safety's sake —
and what I said was strong and sure,
but I didn't say very much at all

and if I got kicked in the teeth
it seemed like pearls would spill out
but they didn't

so I bit my lip
clenched my teeth, swallowed my pride
ate my words, found a voice,
made a name for myself —
and it's on the tip of my tongue

Sean Taylor

names

Today my best pal, my best friend
called me a dirty darkie
When I wouldn't give her a sweetie.
I said, softly, 'I would never believe
you of all people, Char Hardy,
would say that disgusting word to me.
Other children, yes, the ones
that are stupid and ignorant,
and don't know better, but
not you, Char Hardy, not you.
I thought I could trust you.
I never in all the world
expected that word from you.'

Char went a very strange colour.
Said a most peculiar 'Sorry',
as if she was swallowing her voice.
Grabbed me, hugged me, begged me
to forgive her. She was crying.
'I didn't mean it. I didn't mean it.
Honestly. Forgive me. Forgive me.'
I felt the playground sink.
A seesaw rocked, crazy, all by itself.
An orange swing swung high on its own.
My voice was hard as a steel frame:
'Well then, what exactly did you mean?'

Jackie Kay

ATTENTION SEEKING

I'm needing attention.
I know I'm needing attention
because I hear people say it.
People that know these things.
I'm needing attention
so what I'll do is steal something.
I know I'll steal something
because that is what I do
when I need attention.
Or else I mess up my sister's room
throw all her clothes onto the floor
put her hamster under her pillow
and lay a trap above the door
a big heavy dictionary to drop on her
when she comes through. Swot.
This is the kind of thing I do
when I'm needing attention.
But I'm never boring.
I always think up new things.
Attention has lots of colours.
And tunes. And lots of punishments.
For attention you can get detention.
Extra homework. Extra housework.
All sorts of things. Although
yesterday I heard the woman say
to my dad that I was just needing
someone to listen. My dad went mad.
'Listen to him,' he said. 'Listen!
You've got to be joking.'
Mind you that was right after
I stole his car keys and drove
his car straight into the wall.
I wasn't hurt, but I'm still
needing quite a lot of attention.

Jackie Kay

Brendon Gallacher

(For my brother Maxie)

He was seven and I was six, my Brendon Gallacher.
He was Irish and I was Scottish, my Brendon
 Gallacher.
His father was in prison; he was a cat burglar.
My father was a communist party full-time worker.
He had six brothers and I had one, my Brendon
 Gallacher.

He would hold my hand and take me by the river
Where we'd talk all about his family being poor.
He'd get his mum out of Glasgow when he got older.
A wee holiday some place nice. Some place far.
I'd tell my mum about Brendon Gallacher.

How his mum drank and his daddy was a cat burglar.
And she'd say why not have him round to dinner.
No, no, I'd say, he's got big holes in his trousers.
I like to meet him by the burn in the open air.
Then one day after we'd been friends two years

One day when it was pouring and I was indoors,
My mum says to me: I was talking to Mrs Moir
Who lives next door to your Brendon Gallacher.
Didn't you say his address was 24 Novar?
She says there are no Gallachers at 24 Novar

There never have been any Gallachers next door.
And he died then, my Brendon Gallacher
Flat out on the bedroom floor, his spiky hair,
His impish grin, his funny flapping ear.
Oh Brendon. Oh my Brendon Gallacher.

Jackie Kay

from the BIG Sister POEMS ⊙

The Message

Little brother I got a message for you
not from Santa no
It's from Da.
Listen will you.

See before you got born
see Da still had a job to do.
We got bacon and eggs for breakfast.
Ma used to afford to get a hair-do.

Then she goes and gets pregnant again
and even although it was by accident
Da said we could maybe still afford it.
He meant you.

It turns out we can't.

The other thing is
this room before you came along
only had the one bed in it.
Mine.

See there isn't really room for the two.
So what with one thing and another
and since you were the last to arrive
Da says you've to go little brother.

Here is your bag it's packed ready
with your Beanos, pyjamas and a few
biscuits for when you get hungry
I'm sure you'll be better off wherever

you end up so good luck and
goodbye.

The Visitors

Little brother you'll never guess what.
The aliens have just landed.
No they don't have pointed ears
but they are armed and handed.

No they don't have suckers.
No not red blue yellow or green.
But all in black and silver
and one keeps a talking machine

in a special secret pocket.
You can see the blue light out there
well it comes from their rocket.
You can hear their voices downstairs

they're talking to Da that's right.
They want to know where he was
on the planet Earth last night
between seven and ten because

how should I know?
Ma says they'll go away soon
but if you ask me I don't think so.
I think they'll take Da to the moon.

No they are not friendly.
No you can't go downstairs.
I will protect you don't worry.
Move over.

The Warning

Little brother beware the black car
with the strangers' faces in its windows –
the one they call the Getaway Waggon
taking Da to the job he goes.

Little brother beware the black car
with the iron bars in its windows –
the one they call the Black Maria
taking Da to the jail he goes.

Little brother beware the black car
with the dark glass in all its windows –
the one they call the Funeral Hearse
taking Da to the grave he goes.

Little brother beware the black car
no matter what is in its windows
no matter what they call it
taking Da to wherever he goes.

One day it will come for you.

Brian McCabe

nice man

'I'm straightforward, no devices.
I'm not greedy. I give slices.
I'm as nice as nice as nice is.

Trust me, trust me,' he entices.
'Would I roll you loaded dices?
No! I'm as nice as nice as nice is.

Try my chemicals and my spices.
Once is not as good as twice is.
I'm as nice as nice as nice is.

Show me habits. Bring me vices.
See me smile and pay my prices.
I'm as nice as nice as nice is.

Touch me . . . I'm so NICE!
Touch me . . . I'm as cold as ice is.
I'm as nice as nice as nice is.'

Nick Toczek

WHEN YOU'RE OLD

There's so much to do
and it's all set up for you
when you're old . . .

There's clothing arranging
and biscuit exchanging
and pet karaoke
and jam hokey-cokey

embroidery ringing
and cookery singing
and postal aerobics
for tupperware phobics

decorative scissors
and domino quizzes
and hairstyling strimmers
and customised zimmers

collectable swimming
and cross-country slimming
DIY vehicles
and wind-surfing circles

OAP spitting
and radio knitting
with bowling-green jumbles
and Mills and Boon crumbles

community mopping
and memory shopping

the raffia morning
and macramé pawning

and whist bring-and-buys
and cat apple pies
long hours of amateur rheumatics
with nice-cup-of-tea aerobatics . . .

. . . and I'm sure it'd all be amusing
if it wasn't so bloody confusing
when you're old.

Nick Toczek

i wanna be yours

let me be your vacuum cleaner
breathing in your dust
let me be your ford cortina
i will never rust
if you like your coffee hot
let me be your coffee pot
you call the shots
i wanna be yours

let me be your raincoat
for those frequent rainy days
let me be your dreamboat
when you wanna sail away
let me be your teddy bear
take me with you anywhere
i don't care
i wanna be yours

let me be your electric meter
i will not run out
let me be the electric heater
you get cold without
let me be your setting lotion
hold your hair
with deep devotion
deep as the deep
atlantic ocean
that's how deep is my emotion
deep deep deep deep de deep deep
i don't wanna be hers
i wanna be yours

John Cooper Clarke

O O O O O

i don't wanna be nice

here he comes now
the fat fingers the expert eyes
the same old how d'you do
disgust is just his dumb disguise
he wants a word with you
his problems are the end
a mouth needs exercise
the last thing i need is another friend
i don't wanna be nice

i don't wanna be nice
i think it's clever to swear
i would seek some sound advice
but i would look elsewhere
what you see is what you get
you only live twice
a friend in need is a friend in debt
i don't wanna be nice

no we never met before
i'm happy to say
far from perfect strangers
i like to keep it that way
i'm not your psychoanalyst
i'd rather talk to mice
you're so easy to resist
i don't wanna be nice

i don't wanna be nice
i think it's clever to swear

i would seek some sound advice
but i would look elsewhere
your face is an obvious case
you shouldn't put it about
this is neither the time nor place
to sort these matters out
what you see is what you get
you only live twice
a friend in need is a friend in debt
i don't wanna be nice

John Cooper Clarke

LAW OF OPPOSITES

Try to overstand
Said de lawd
of creation
That de earth
is not fulla contradiction
It's just the way
I planned it
Yuh see de earth
is governed by de
Law of opposite.

De opposite to Jah
is Satan
De opposite to Man
is a Woman
De opposite to Beast
is Human
De opposite to Sea
must be Land
De Sun de Moon
De Stars in de Sky
these are de works
of de Almighty I.

De opposite to Good
dat is Bad
De opposite to Happy
dat is Sad
De opposite to Sane
mean yuh Mad
One of these emotions
wi all have had
Now they might seem negative

Negative
But then they could
be positive
There's two side to
everyting so let's
go on with the reasonin.

De opposite to War
dat is Peace
De opposite to de West
is de East
De opposite to Wrong
yes dat's Right
De opposite to Black
dat is White
De opposite to Beautiful
is Ugly
De opposite to Free
is Captivity
De Opposite to Wealthy
is Poverty
De opposite to a Friend
is an Enemy
LOVE is a good remedy
It's been dat way since
Antiquity.

De opposite ti Ill Health
is Hearty
De opposite to Lightweight
Happens to be Heavy
De opposite to Smooth
Dat is Rough
De opposite to Tender
dat is Tough
Hot and Cold
Wet and Dry
Young and Old
De Truth a Lie
De opposite to Short
dat is Long
De opposite to Weak

dat is Strong
And suh I could
go on and on
but now yuh should a
learnt de lesson
There is only two vibrations
Negative and Positive
De opposite to Life
dat is Death
It's just dat Death
Hasn't received you yet.

Levi Tafari

Sense outta Nansense

di innocent an di fool could paas fi twin
but haas a haas
an mule a mule
mawgah mean mawgah
it noh mean slim

yet di two a dem in camman share someting

dem is awftin canfused an get used
dem is awftin criticised an campramised
dem is awftin villified an reviled
dem is awftin foun guilty widoutn being tried

wan ting set di two a dem far apawt dow
di innocent wi hawbah dout
check tings out
an maybe fine out
but di fool
cho . . .

di innocent an di fool could paas fi twin
but like a like
an love a love
a pidgin is a pidgin
an a dove is a dove

yet di two a dem in camman share someting

dem is awftin anticipated an laywaited
dem is awftin patronised an penalised
dem is awftin pacified an isolated
dem is awftin castigated and implicated

wan ting set di two a dem far apawt dow
di innocent wi hawbah dout
check tings out

an maybe fine out
but di fool
cho . . .

di innocent and di fool could paas fi twin
but rat a rat
an mouse a mouse
flea a flea
an louse a louse

yet di two a dem in camman share someting

dem is awftin decried an denied
dem is awftin ridiculed an doungraded
dem is sometimes kangratulated an celebrated
dem is sometimes suprised an elated
but as yu mite have already guess
dem is awftin fouri wantin more or less

dus spoke di wizen wans af ole
dis is a story nevvah told

Linton Kwesi Johnson

fourth generation

not part of this nation
a creation
of divided nation
our generation
fighting for recognition
music and war
come before
salvation
kids on the streets
drumming beats
knowing it gets harder
the more you push
the more they pull
'til it becomes die or kill

Fourth generation
living between double nation
crossing the cease-fire line
before time
it's a hard situation
fighting for love
it comes from up above
salvation our generation
in love with war
can't take no more
fighting for change
money in my pocket
loose change
chatting in school
playing pool
it's time for home rule
break the rules
they're the fools
we're the cools
tell us we got no tools
in our heads

and they're the deads
dead beat rhythm in the street
dancing on ice
cool beat
doing Bhangra
with out feet
the Samosa Kids
are in town
chillies and masala
when you're down
skin is brown
don't frown
we're your friends
won't bring you down
come around
the beat's in town
Bhangra beat
won't bring you down
come around
the beat's in town
Bhangra beat
won't bring you down
Johnny Z
will set you free
follow me
the rule breakers
are escaping
the language makers
are saying
come and join
come and find
set free your mind
don't be blind

Fourth generation
our nation
will find a beat
heart beat.

Maya Chowdhry

nothing for girls

(For Angela)

First there is the childsong,
bright blue childsong,
ringing up the air.
You are the sky
and the bird and the cloud
and the scruffy earth
and the mole and the worm
and the world is all people.

Then there is the difference.
Rainbow childsong.
Colours have a place.
You still put faces
on the trees and mushrooms
but you begin to see borders,
where the sky, where play ends,
school begins.

Borders build a world.
Here's a country for under-twelves.
Here's the teenage nation.
There's the adult set,
they're called 'people'.
Children are sort of apprentice people,
so they don't understand,
so they have all these notions
about things being people
and colours having faces
and sums being boring
and they hate borders.

. . . and people kind of envy um
although they say they love um
and there's another thing
although they say they love um
they're always trying to change um
more like children love people
because they become like um. . .

Children never understand
why people feel so bitter.
I mean, that's what children aim for —
to be people.
But people are always sorry
they can't be children again.
Because when you're people
you must believe in borders
and don't believe your eyes
or your ears or anything you feel.

There's a little girl
who runs and shouts
and turns cartwheels
and wants to be an artist
and takes on all the boys
and beats them and loves it.
Doesn't see tomboy.
Doesn't see girl-not-boy
Doesn't see boy-not-girl
Sees people —
                in a cartwheel
                in a colour
                in a sweat
                in a treat

people hugging
people crying
people almost split from laughing
people people people . . .

There she is
in the comic shop
looking for herself
and sees nothing but borders,
what she is not,
what they are,
and suddenly she changes.
'Nothing,' she says, head down,
'Nothing for girls.'

Máighréad Medbh

End Of A Free Ride

For years
my cousin never charged me
on the bus.

One day he said to my sister,
'Your wan would need to watch herself
stickin' up for the knackers,'

After that he went home
and had pig's cheek and cabbage
lemon swiss roll and tea.

He called out to his wife Annie,
(who was in the scullery steeping
the shank for Thursday)

'Annie love get us the milk,
was I telling' ya,
I'll have to start chargin' my cousin
full fare from here on in.'

'Why's that?' said Annie love
returning with the milk

'Cos she's an adult now, that's why.'

Rita Ann Higgins

BE SOMEONE

(For Carmel)

For Christ's sake,
learn to type
and have something
to fall back on.

Be someone,
make something of yourself,
look at Gertrudo Ganley.

Always draw the curtains
when the lights are on.

Have nothing to do
with the Shantalla gang,
get yourself a right man
with a Humber Sceptre.

For Christ's sake
wash your neck
before going into God's house.

Learn to speak properly,
always pronounce your ings.
Never smoke on the street,
don't be caught dead
in them shameful tight slacks,

spare the butter,
economize,

and for Christ's sake
at all times,
watch your language.

Rita Ann Higgins

blue coffee

Blue coffee
The air was like
Blue coffee

Frothy cow's parsley
Either side of the path
Across the Heath

Blue coffee
The whirling air was like
Blue coffee

Up jumped a poppy in scarlet
Her heart beating black as the blues

Blue coffee
The swirling, spiralling air
Blue coffee

Adrian Mitchell

a flying song

(For Caitlin Georgia Isabel Stubbs
April 18th, 1993)

Last night I saw the sword Excalibur
It flew above the cloudy palaces
And as it passed I clearly read the words
Which were engraven on its blade
   And one side of the sword said 'Take Me'
   The other side said 'Cast Me Away.'

I met my lover in a field of thorns
We walked together in the April air
And when we lay down by the waterside
My lover whispered in my ear
   The first thing that she said was 'Take Me'
   The last thing that she said was 'Cast Me Away.'

I saw a vision of my mother and father
They were sitting smiling under summer trees
They offered me the gift of life
I took this present very carefully
   And one side of my life said 'Take Me'
   The other side said 'Cast Me Away.'

Adrian Mitchell

YES

A smile says: Yes.
A heart says: Blood.
When the rain says: Drink.
The earth says: Mud.

The kangaroo says: Trampoline.
Giraffes say: Tree.
A bus says: Us,
While a car says: Me.

Lemon trees say: Lemons.
A jug says: Lemonade.

The villain says: You're wonderful,
The hero: I'm afraid.

The forest says: Hide and Seek.
The grass says: Green and Grow.
The railway says: Maybe.
The prison says: No.

The millionaire says: Take.
The beggar says: Give.
The soldier cries: Mother!
The baby sings: Live.

The river says: Come with me.
The moon says: Bless.
The stars say: Enjoy the light.
The sun says: Yes.

Adrian Mitchell

How Laughter Helped Stop the Argument

FIRST VOICE: Look at the clouds
so fluffy
so sheepy
That's because God
got woolly hair.

SECOND VOICE: Look at the rain
falling strands
falling everywhere
That's because God
got straight hair.

THIRD VOICE: Look at de sun
look at de moon
That's why
God's got a yellow eye.

FOURTH VOICE: Look at the sea
look at the sky
That's a clue
God's skin must be blue.

FIFTH VOICE: What about the night
that wraps us dark
and makes us sleep tight?
God's skin must be black.

SIXTH VOICE: What about the snow?
Oh no, God's skin must be
white.

THIRD VOICE: No, God's skin must be green
look at de trees
See what I mean.

FIRST VOICE: Well, then since you are all so
clever

just answer me
Is God a father or a mother?

SECOND VOICE: A father.

FIFTH VOICE: A mother.

SIXTH VOICE: No, a father.

THIRD VOICE: How about a grandmother?

AND WHILE THESE SIX VOICES
WERE ARGUING AND ARGUING
JUST THEN A SEVENTH VOICE STEPPED IN

Listen my friends
and listen well
crick me your ears
and I'll crack you a spell

God might be a story
with no beginning
and no end

God might be laughter
for all you know
God might be a HA – HA – HA – HAaaaaaaaaaaa
        a HO – HO – HO – HOoooooooooooo
        a HE – HE – HE – HEeeeeeeeeee
        a SHE – SHE – SHE – SHEeeeeeeeeeeee

        a million million
        laughing pebbles
        inside of
            you and me

    That's what God might be.

John Agard

COWTALK

Take a walk to the splendid morning fields of summer
check out the cows in full gleam
of their black and white hide

and remember was a man once say I have a dream
but they shoot him down in cold blood of day
because he had a mountaintop dream
of black and white hand in hand

take a walk to the splendid morning fields of summer
check out the cows in green of meditation
a horde of black and white harmony

maybe the cows trying to tell us something
but we the human butchers can't understand cowtalk
much less cowsilence
to interpret cowsilence you must send for a poet
not a butcher or a politician

cows in the interwoven glory
of their black and white hide
have their own mysterious story
cows in the interwoven glory
of their black and white hide
never heard of apartheid
never practise genocide
never seem to worry
that the grass greener on the other side
cows calmly marry and intermarry

cows in the interwoven glory
of their black and white hide
cows in the interwoven glory
of black and white integration
can't spell integration
cows never went to school
that's why cows so cool supercool
cows have little time for immigration rule
and above all cows never impose
their language on
another nation

do yoo moo my message/do yoo moo
moo my message/moo
do yoo moo my message/do yoo moo
moo my message/moo

John Agard

O

THIS POEM

I wish this poem *bon voyage*:
may it be read with delight
by whoever shall sail in her.

May it traverse the oceans
to all peoples irrespective
of colour, creed, language,

or a pious belief in poetry.
May it carry hints of beauty
in spaces between its words,

and impart its love of life
to those with ears to hear.
May it negotiate rough seas

of cynicism and not flounder
on rocks of scholarliness.
To avoid doldrums, may it

never be recited at school,
nor used for exam purposes.
This poem is to be enjoyed.

It has no other function.
Neither epic nor symbolic,
it does not refer to myth.

No interpretation is needed,
nor are there any footnotes.
This poem says what it means.

May it never be the property
of anyone, may no one ever
force a commentary upon it.

May it never be captured
by propaganda pirates,
nor put to commercial use.

May it beach only on a shore
where logic has been outcast
by the language of the heart.

Norman Silver